BULLDOZER's
Big

Candace Fleming and Eric

Atheneum Atheneum Books for Young Readers

Day

Rohmann

New York London Toronto Sydney New Delhi

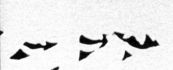  

It was Bulldozer's big day.

And he couldn't wait to invite all his friends to his party.

Motor humming and blade held high, he zoomed—
bump-vroom—across the construction site.

"Guess what today is!" whooped Bulldozer when he got to where Digger Truck was working.

"Guess?" Digger boomed. "I don't need to guess, kid. Today is a scooping day. Scooping . . . scooping . . . scooping."

"And a sifting day,"
Dump Truck rumbled.
"Sifting . . . sifting . . . sifting."

Bulldozer's blade drooped a little.

He rolled to where Cement Mixer was working.

"Guess what today is?"
called Bulldozer.

"I already know,"
Cement Mixer belched.
"Today is a stirring day.
Stirring . . . stirring . . .
stirring."

And Bulldozer's blade drooped a bit lower.

He rumbled to where Scraper and Grader were working.

"Guess what—" began Bulldozer.

"Guess?" Scraper rattled. "Who has time to guess?
Today is a filling day. Filling . . . filling . . . filling."

"And a chopping day," Grader clattered. "Chopping . . .
chopping . . . chopping."

And Bulldozer's blade drooped lower still.

He bumped to where Roller Truck was working.

"Do you care what today is?" asked Bulldozer.

"No," Roller grumbled. With a hiss of smoke, he huffed away. "Mashing day," he muttered. "Mashing . . . mashing . . . mashing."

And Bulldozer's blade drooped so low,
it almost touched the ground.

He crawled to where Crane Truck was working.

"I don't suppose *you* know what today is,"
Bulldozer said with a sigh.

"Of course I do," Crane clanged.

"You do?" asked Bulldozer. His blade
rose hopefully.

"It's a lifting day," Crane banged.
"Lifting . . . lifting . . . lifting.
And *this* is my sixth and last—"

Wooot!
The construction whistle blew.

Bulldozer turned away, his blade dragging sadly in the dirt.
"No games." He sniffled. "No friends. No party."

Then—

Feeef!
A different kind of whistle blew.
Tooot! Hoooot! Wooooo!

Lots of whistles blew.

"You do know what today is!" cried Bulldozer.

And as his friends revved their engines
and honked their horns,
Bulldozer raised his blade high . . .

. . . and made a wish.

"Hooray!" blared the others.

Then Bulldozer squealed, "What are we waiting for? Let's dig in."

And they did!

For David Andrew...vroom-vroom! —C. F.

For the Crusty Nibs —E. R.

atheneum

ATHENEUM BOOKS FOR YOUNG READERS
An imprint of Simon & Schuster Children's Publishing Division
1230 Avenue of the Americas, New York, New York 10020
Text copyright © 2015 by Candace Fleming
Illustrations copyright © 2015 by Eric Rohmann
All rights reserved, including the right of reproduction in whole or in
part in any form.
ATHENEUM BOOKS FOR YOUNG READERS is a registered trademark of
Simon & Schuster, Inc.
Atheneum logo is a trademark of Simon & Schuster, Inc.
For information about special discounts for bulk purchases, please
contact Simon & Schuster Special Sales at 1-866-506-1949 or
business@simonandschuster.com.
The Simon & Schuster Speakers Bureau can bring authors to your live
event. For more information or to book an event, contact the
Simon & Schuster Speakers Bureau at 1-866-248-3049 or visit our
website at www.simonspeakers.com.
Book design by Ann Bobco
The text for this book is set in Futura BT.
The illustrations for this book were made using relief (block) prints.
Three plates were used for each image. The first two plates were
printed in multiple colors, using a relief printmaking process called
"reduction printing." The last plate was the "key" image, which was
printed in black over the color.
Manufactured in China
0215 SCP
First Edition
10 9 8 7 6 5 4 3 2 1
Library of Congress Cataloging-in-Publication Data
Fleming, Candace.
Bulldozer's big day / Candace Fleming ; illustrated by Eric Rohmann.
— First edition.
p. cm
ISBN 978-1-4814-0097-8 (hardcover)
ISBN 978-1-4814-0098-5 (eBook)
[1. Bulldozers—Fiction. 2. Construction equipment—Fiction.
3. Birthdays—Fiction. 4. Parties—Fiction.] I. Rohmann, Eric, illustrator.
II. Title.
PZ7.F59936Bul 2015
[E]—dc23
2013038526